Dream Beans

written by
Betsy Church

illustrated by
David Molinero

Copyright © 2021 by Betsy Reese Church

Publisher's Cataloging-in-Publication data

Names: Church, Betsy, author. | Molinero, David, illustrator.

Title: Dream beans / by Betsy Church ; illustrated by David Molinero.

Description: Cumming, GA: Dream Beans Publishing, 2021. | Summary: Oscar shares his discovery of "Dream Beans," a metaphor for the Fruit of the Spirit: Love, Joy, Peace, Patience, Kindness, Goodness, Faithfulness, Gentleness and Self-Control.

Identifiers: LCCN: 2021911757 | ISBN: 978-1-7369828-0-8 (hardcover) | 978-1-7369828-1-5 (paperback) | 978-1-7369828-2-2 (ebook)

Subjects: LCSH Fruit of the Spirit—Juvenile fiction. | Emotions—Juvenile fiction. | Christian fiction. | Family—Juvenile fiction. | CYAC Fruit of the Spirit—Fiction. | Emotions—Fiction. | Family—Fiction. | BISAC JUVENILE FICTION / Religious / Christian / Bedtime & Dreams | JUVENILE FICTION / Religious / Christian / Learning Concepts | JUVENILE FICTION / Religious / Christian / Emotions & Feelings

Classification: LCC PZ7.1.C52 Dre 2021 | DDC [E]--dc23

Layout and Design by Louie Romares

All rights reserved. This book or any portion thereof may not be reproduced or used in any manner whatsoever without the express written permission of the author.

This book belongs to:

_____

Dear Reader,

God wrote this story on my heart and later revealed to me that Dream Beans is a metaphor for the Fruit of the Spirit: Love, Joy, Peace, Patience, Kindness, Goodness, Faithfulness, Gentleness and Self-Control. With a wink and a nod to that idea, look for the tiny fruit on the front pocket of each Dream Bean.

My hope is that this story will give you the feeling of being wrapped in a warm blanket of Peace, Joy and Possibility.

With love and gratitude,

Betsy Church

I dedicate this book to you,

Dear Reader.

May it help you to feel infinitely

loved.

A boy goes to bed with some thoughts in his head…
As he drifts off to sleep, a tiny voice speaks…
"Oscar…Oscar…Can you hear me?"
"What was that? Who's there?" asks Oscar.
"Please help me!" begs the tiny voice.

"Who are you?" Oscar asks,
turning on his light.
He doesn't see anyone.
Maybe he was just dreaming.

"We are your Dream Beans!
You can't always see us,
but we are here to encourage
and inspire you."

Oscar looks under his bed.

No one is there.

"How did you get here?"

"God planted us in your heart."

"But why?" Oscar asks

The tiny voice answers, "He wants you to know that there is only one YOU in the whole wide world.

He gave you special gifts and talents so you could be your best YOU and do the things that only YOU can do!"

"But I'm just little," Oscar replies, crawling back into his bed. "I can't do big things yet."

"Remember that big hug you gave your mother yesterday? That was something only YOU can do. Your hug meant a lot to your mom!

"And remember when you were cheering for your best friend when he was trying to ride his bike—and he was really discouraged because he fell off?"

"Yes, I remember," says Oscar.

"Those were important things that YOU did," says the voice.

Oscar thinks for a few minutes.

"Oh, okay, so is there something you want me to do?" he finally asks.

"Yes, you can tell your mom and dad and all your friends about us. Then they can listen for THEIR Dream Beans too, and learn about their gifts and talents and what they can do to make THEIR dreams come true."

"Okay," Oscar agrees. " I will tell them.

As Oscar drifts back to sleep, he dreams about the Dream Beans. He hears the tiny voice speaking to him.

When morning comes, Oscar runs to tell his dad about the Dream Beans.

"What if Dad doesn't believe me?" he worries.

"Dad, I have something important to share with you,"

Oscar says, "I found my Dream Beans. Well, actually they found me."

Dad was busy working at his computer. "I'm sorry buddy," he said.

"I'm too busy right now. I have too much work to do."

"But Dad," Oscar begs, "they are here to help me be my best ME.

God also planted them in YOUR heart, so you can be YOUR best YOU.

"That's nice, son, but I don't have time to listen to you," Dad says, as he turns back to his computer.

"Okay, I can see that you are busy. I will come back later."

Oscar walks slowly back to his room, feeling sad.

He slips under his blanket and closes his eyes.

"Dream Beans, are you still here?" he asks quietly.

A tiny voice answers, "We are here and will always be with you.

Don't be discouraged.

Just share the message and leave the rest to us."

Oscar goes to tell his mom.

"Mom, I have something important to share! I found my Dream Beans, or they found me, and they are here to help me be my best ME! God planted Dream Beans in YOUR heart too, so you can be YOUR best YOU!"

Mom looks up and smiles.

"Do you get it, Mom?
Do you see them, too?"

"Yes, thank you, buddy," she says. "I do see them—especially early in the morning as I sit on the porch in my favorite chair.

They are right here with me enjoying this beautiful day. I lost them for a while, but now I've found them again and it's great to see them. They are like long lost friends. But now I do…I do see them."

"Did they help you, Mom?" Oscar asks.

"Yes, they helped me with my writing, my sewing and even my dancing.

They helped me figure out what is mine to do!"

Oscar can't wait to tell his friends.

"You can take it or leave it, that's up to you," he says to Matilda and Jack, "but believe it or not, you ALL have Dream Beans."

"God made mine for ME and He made yours special for YOU. That's because He wants me to be ME and you to be YOU."

"All you have to do is listen to your Dream Beans and they will help you see that you can be anything you want to be. YOU can make your dreams come true."

Oscar felt good about spreading the word.

He decided to talk to his dad again.

"Dad," he said, "I know you are busy and stressed and working hard, but can you please take a break and eat dinner with me?"

Dad put his papers down, turned off his computer and looked at his son.

Oscar continued, "Dad, I really appreciate all the stuff you do for us, but you know what I want most? I just want to spend time with you."

Dad looks sad. "I'm sorry I have been too busy for you," he says.

"Tell me again what you want me to do."

"I want you to know about your Dream Beans, Dad" Oscar answers.

"I know they can help you. Do you see them? Do you hear them?"

"No, not yet. How do I do that?" Dad asks.

Oscar explains. "You have to get really still and quiet, and close your eyes.

Then you can ask your Dream Beans about God, or you can ask God about your Dream Beans.

But to hear them, you have to get rid of distractions—like computers and papers.

Nature is a really great place to find them.

Oscar asks Dad the most important question of all.

"Dad, what is something you have always dreamed of doing?"

Dad closes his eyes and thinks for a minute.

"While this may sound silly," he says as he opens his eyes, "I have always dreamed of going fishing. I could just never find the time."

"Dad, can we make that happen for you?"

Oscar asks, "Can we make one of your dreams come true—together?"

"Yes Buddy. Thank you!"

Oscar knows that nothing will ever be as special as today. He is helping his dad make one of HIS dreams come true.

As Oscar and his dad sit on the dock, their feet dangling in the water, Dad suddenly looks up and points to a faraway spot across the river.

"Look son!" he shouts.

"Do you see them? Do you see what I see?"

It's a lot more simple than it seems...

to listen to the voices of your Dream Beans.

Each of them has something to say...

and all are important to show us the way!

Author Betsy Church has a B.S. degree in Education and is proud to consider herself a lifelong learner. She has a passion for helping others to see their potential, and finds honor and privilege in encouraging them to be the best they can be.

Hi Friend,

Thank you for reading Dream Beans. I hope my words will inspire each and every child who hears them, and open their hearts and minds to All that God has for us.

I would love to connect with you and your children and share some free resources. You can find the information at thedreambeans.com

If you see the value this book adds to kids' lives, please leave an honest review on Amazon. Your review will help others learn about the book and will encourage me to keep writing.

Blessings to you and yours,

Betsy Church

"May the God of hope fill you with all joy and peace in believing, so that you may abound in hope by the power of the Holy Spirit."

Romans 15:13

New King James Version

Meet Dream

Love

Joy

Peace

Patience

the Beans

Self-Control

Kindness

Goodness

Faithfulness

Gentleness

CPSIA information can be obtained
at www.ICGtesting.com
Printed in the USA
BVHW020419221122
651512BV00004B/14